STAY AWAY, GERMS

By Monique McDaniel

Illustrated by Mikel Holloway

Archway Publishing books may be ordered through booksellers or by contacting:

Archway Publishing
1663 Liberty Drive
Bloomington, IN 47403
www.archwaypublishing.com
844.669.3957

Interior Image Credit: Mikel Holloway

ISBN: 978-1-4808-9647-5 (sc)
ISBN: 978-1-4808-9648-2 (e)

Print information available on the last page.

Archway Publishing rev. date: 10/01/2020

STAY AWAY, GERMS

My name is Kringe.
I am a nasty germ.

My name is Bailey.
Let's talk about germs.

Germs can be near.

Germs can be far.

Germs can be wherever you are.

My name is Ali.

Let's wash our hands.

Clean up when you come in from play.

Use soap and water to wash the germs away.

Now it's your turn to wash away germs.

My name is Kia.

I clean my room, and so should you.

Clean up.

Be smart; be wise!

Clean up; clean up.

Germs can't hide.

My name is Summer.

Don't forget your mask.

Take your new cover
as you go out today.

Wear a mask to keep
the germs away.

Can you help us keep
the germs away?

Help us find a cure
today, and make those
germs stay away!